THE ADVOCATE'S WEDDING-DAY.

BY CATHERINE CROWE.

Antoine de Chaulieu was the son of a poor gentleman of Normandy, with a long genealogy, a short rent-roll, and a large family. Jacques Rollet was the son of a brewer, who did not know who his grandfather was; but he had a long purse, and only two children. As these youths flourished in the early days of liberty, equality, and fraternity, and were near neighbors, they naturally hated each other. Their enmity commenced at school, where the delicate and refined De Chaulieu, being the only *gentilhomme* amongst the scholars, was the favorite of the master (who was a bit of an aristocrat in his heart), although he was about the worst dressed boy in the establishment, and never had a sou to spend; whilst Jacques Rollet, sturdy and rough, with smart clothes and plenty of money, got flogged six days in the week, ostensibly for being stupid and not learning his lessons,—which he did not,—but in reality for constantly quarrelling with and insulting De Chaulieu, who had not strength to cope with him.

When they left the academy, the feud continued in all its vigor, and was fostered by a thousand little circumstances, arising out of the state of the times, till a separation ensued, in consequence of an aunt of Antoine de Chaulieu's undertaking the expense of sending him to Paris to study the law, and of maintaining him there during the necessary period.

With the progress of events came some degree of reaction in favor of birth and nobility; and then Antoine, who had passed for the bar, began to hold up his head, and endeavor to push his fortunes; but fate seemed against him. He felt certain that if he possessed any gift in the world, it was that of eloquence, but he could get no cause to plead; and his aunt dying inopportunely, first his resources failed, and then his health. He had no sooner returned to his home than, to complicate his difficulties completely, he fell in love with Miss Natalie de Bellefonds, who had just returned from Paris, where she had been completing her education. To expatiate on the perfections of Mademoiselle Natalie would be a waste of ink and paper; it is sufficient to say that she really was a very charming girl, with a fortune which, though not large, would have been a most desirable addition to De Chaulieu, who had nothing. Neither was the fair Natalie indisposed to listen to his addresses; but her father could not be expected to countenance the suit of a gentleman, however well-born, who had not a ten-sous piece in the world, and whose prospects were a blank.

Whilst the ambitious and love-sick barrister was thus pining in unwelcome obscurity, his old acquaintance, Jacques Rollet, had been acquiring an undesirable notoriety. There was nothing really bad in Jacques; but having been bred up a democrat, with a hatred of the nobility, he could not easily accommodate his rough humor to treat them with civility when it was no longer safe to insult them. The liberties he allowed himself whenever circumstances brought him into contact with the higher classes of society, had led him into many scrapes, out of which his father's money had in one way or another released him; but that source of safety had now failed. Old Rollet, having been too busy with the affairs of the nation to attend to his business, had died insolvent, leaving his son with nothing but his own wits to help him out of future difficulties; and it was not long before their exercise was called for.

Claudine Rollet, his sister, who was a very pretty girl, had attracted the attention of Mademoiselle de Bellefonds's brother, Alphonse; and as he paid her more attention than from such a quarter was agreeable to Jacques, the young men had had more than one quarrel on the subject, on which occasion they had each, characteristically, given vent to their enmity, the one in contemptuous monosyllables, and the other in a volley of insulting words. But Claudine had another lover, more nearly of her own condition of life; this was Claperon, the deputy-governor of the Rouen jail, with whom she had made acquaintance during one or two compulsory visits paid by her brother to that functionary. Claudine, who was a bit of a coquette, though she did not altogether reject his suit, gave him little encouragement, so that, betwixt hopes and fears and doubts and jealousies, poor Claperon led a very uneasy kind of life.

Affairs had been for some time in this position, when, one fine morning, Alphonse de Bellefonds was not to be found in his chamber when his servant went to call him; neither had his bed been slept in. He had been observed to go out rather late on the previous evening, but whether he had returned nobody could tell. He had not appeared at supper, but that was too ordinary an event to awaken suspicion; and little alarm was excited till several hours had elapsed, when inquiries were instituted and a search commenced, which terminated in the discovery of his body, a good deal mangled, lying at the bottom of a pond which had belonged to the old brewery.

Before any investigation had been made, every person had jumped to the conclusion that the young man had been murdered, and that Jacques Rollet was the assassin. There was a strong presumption in favor of that opinion, which further perquisitions tended to confirm. Only the day before, Jacques had been heard to threaten Monsieur de Bellefonds with speedy vengeance. On the fatal evening, Alphonse and Claudine had been seen together in the neighborhood of the now dismantled brewery; and as Jacques, betwixt poverty and democracy, was in bad odor with the respectable part of society, it was not easy for him to bring witnesses to character or to prove an unexceptionable *alibi*. As for the Bellefonds and De Chaulieus, and the aristocracy in general, they entertained no doubt of his guilt; and finally, the magistrates coming to the same opinion, Jacques Rollet was committed for trial at the next assizes, and as a testimony of good-will, Antoine de Chaulieu was selected by the injured family to conduct the prosecution.

Here, at last, was the opportunity he had sighed for. So interesting a case, too, furnishing such ample occasion for passion, pathos, indignation! And how eminently fortunate that the speech which he set himself with ardor to prepare would be delivered in the presence of the father and brother of his mistress, and perhaps of the lady herself. The evidence against Jacques, it is true, was altogether presumptive; there was no proof whatever that he had committed the crime; and for his own part, he stoutly denied it. But Antoine de Chaulieu entertained no doubt of his guilt, and the speech he composed was certainly well calculated to carry that conviction into the bosom of others. It was of the highest importance to his own reputation that he should procure a verdict, and he confidently assured the afflicted and enraged family of the victim that their vengeance should be satisfied.

Under these circumstances, could anything be more unwelcome than a piece of intelligence that was privately conveyed to him late on the evening before the trial was to come on, which tended strongly to exculpate the prisoner, without indicating any other person as the criminal. Here was an opportunity lost. The first step of the ladder on which he was to rise to fame, fortune, and a wife was slipping from under his feet.

Of course so interesting a trial was anticipated with great eagerness by the public; the court was crowded with all the beauty and fashion of Rouen, and amongst the rest, doubly interesting in her mourning, sat the fair Natalie, accompanied by her family.

The young advocate's heart beat high; he felt himself inspired by the occasion; and although

Jacques Rollet persisted in asserting his innocence, founding his defence chiefly on circumstances which were strongly corroborated by the information that had reached De Chaulieu the preceding evening, he was nevertheless convicted.

In spite of the very strong doubts he privately entertained respecting the justice of the verdict, even De Chaulieu himself, in the first flush of success, amidst a crowd of congratulating friends and the approving smiles of his mistress, felt gratified and happy; his speech had, for the time being, not only convinced others but himself; warmed with his own eloquence, he believed what he said. But when the glow was over, and he found himself alone, he did not feel so comfortable. A latent doubt of Rollet's guilt now pressed strongly on his mind, and he felt that the blood of the innocent would be on his head. It was true there was yet time to save the life of the prisoner; but to admit Jacques innocent, was to take the glory out of his own speech, and turn the sting of his argument against himself. Besides, if he produced the witness who had secretly given him the information, he should be self-condemned, for he could not conceal that he had been aware of the circumstance before the trial.

Matters having gone so far, therefore, it was necessary that Jacques Rollet should die; and so the affair took its course; and early one morning the guillotine was erected in the court-yard of the gaol, three criminals ascended the scaffold, and three heads fell into the basket, which were presently afterward, with the trunks that had been attached to them, buried in a corner of the cemetery.

Antoine de Chaulieu was now fairly started in his career, and his success was as rapid as the first step toward it had been tardy. He took a pretty apartment in the Hôtel Marbœuf, Rue Grange Batelière, and in a short time was looked upon as one of the most rising young advocates in Paris. His success in one line brought him success in another; he was soon a favorite in society, and an object of interest to speculating mothers; but his affections still adhered to his old love, Natalie de Bellefonds, whose family now gave their assent to the match,—at least prospectively,—a circumstance which furnished such additional incentive to his exertions, that in about two years from his first brilliant speech he was in a sufficiently flourishing condition to offer the young lady a suitable home.

In anticipation of the happy event, he engaged and furnished a suite of apartments in the Rue de Helder; and as it was necessary that the bride should come to Paris to provide her trousseau, it was agreed that the wedding should take place there, instead of at Bellefonds, as had been first projected,—an arrangement the more desirable, that a press of business rendered Monsieur de Chaulieu's absence from Paris inconvenient.

Brides and bridegrooms in France, except of the very high classes, are not much in the habit of making those honeymoon excursions so universal in this country. A day spent in visiting Versailles, or St. Cloud, or even the public places of the city, is generally all that precedes the settling down into the habits of daily life. In the present instance, St. Denis was selected, from the circumstance of Natalie's having a younger sister at school there, and also because she had a particular desire to see the Abbey.

The wedding was to take place on a Thursday; and on the Wednesday evening, having spent some hours most agreeably with Natalie, Antoine de Chaulieu returned to spend his last night in his bachelor apartments. His wardrobe and other small possessions had already been packed up, and sent to his future home; and there was nothing left in his room now but his new wedding suit, which he inspected with considerable satisfaction before he undressed and lay down to sleep.

Sleep, however, was somewhat slow to visit him, and the clock had struck one before he closed his eyes. When he opened them again, it was broad daylight, and his first thought was, had he overslept himself? He sat up in bed to look at the clock, which was exactly opposite; and as he did so, in the large mirror over the fireplace, he perceived a figure standing behind him. As the dilated eyes met his own, he saw it was the face of Jacques Rollet. Overcome with horror, he sank back on his pillow, and it was some minutes before he ventured to look again in that direction; when he did so, the figure had disappeared.

The sudden revulsion of feeling which such a vision was calculated to occasion in a man elate with joy may be conceived. For some time after the death of his former foe, he had been visited by not infrequent twinges of conscience; but of late, borne along by success and the hurry of Parisian life, these unpleasant remembrances had grown rarer, till at length they had faded away altogether. Nothing had been further from his thoughts than Jacques Rollet when he closed his eyes on the preceding night, or when he opened them to that sun which was to shine on what he expected to be the happiest day of his life. Where were the high-strung nerves now, the elastic frame, the bounding heart?

Heavily and slowly he arose from his bed, for it was time to do so; and with a trembling hand and quivering knees he went through the processes of the toilet, gashing his cheek with the razor, and spilling the water over his well-polished boots.

When he was dressed, scarcely venturing to cast a glance in the mirror as he passed it, he quitted the room and descended the stairs, taking the key of the door with him, for the purpose of leaving it with the porter; the man, however, being absent, he laid it on the table in his lodge, and with a relaxed hand and languid step he proceeded to the carriage which quickly conveyed him to the church, where he was met by Natalie and her friends.

How difficult it was now to look happy, with that pallid face and extinguished eye!

"How pale you are! Has anything happened? You are surely ill?" were the exclamations that assailed him on all sides.

He tried to carry the thing off as well as he could, but he felt that the movements he would have wished to appear alert were only convulsive, and that the smiles with which he attempted to relax his features were but distorted grimaces. However, the church was not the place for further inquiries; and whilst Natalie gently pressed his hand in token of sympathy, they advanced to the altar, and the ceremony was performed; after which they stepped into the carriages waiting at the door, and drove to the apartments of Madame de Bellefonds, where an elegant *déjeuner* was prepared.

"What ails you, my dear husband?" inquired Natalie, as soon as they were alone.

"Nothing, love," he replied; "nothing, I assure you, but a restless night and a little overwork, in order that I might have to-day free to enjoy my happiness."

"Are you quite sure? Is there nothing else?"

"Nothing, indeed, and pray don't take notice of it; it only makes me worse."

Natalie was not deceived, but she saw that what he said was true,—notice made him worse; so she contented herself with observing him quietly and saying nothing; but as he felt she was observing him, she might almost better have spoken; words are often less embarrassing things than too curious eyes.

When they reached Madame de Bellefonds' he had the same sort of scrutiny to undergo, till he grew quite impatient under it, and betrayed a degree of temper altogether unusual with him. Then everybody looked astonished; some whispered their remarks, and others expressed them by their wondering eyes, till his brow knit, and his pallid cheeks became flushed with anger.

Neither could he divert attention by eating; his parched mouth would not allow him to swallow anything but liquids, of which he indulged in copious libations; and it was an exceeding relief to him when the carriage which was to convey them to St. Denis, being announced, furnished an excuse for hastily leaving the table.

Looking at his watch, he declared it was late; and Natalie, who saw how eager he was to be gone, threw her shawl over her shoulders, and bidding her friends good morning they hurried away.

It was a fine sunny day in June; and as they drove along the crowded boulevards and through the Porte St. Denis, the young bride and bridegroom, to avoid each other's eyes, affected to be gazing out of the windows; but when they reached that part of the road where there was nothing but trees on each side, they felt it necessary to draw in their heads, and make an attempt at conversation.

De Chaulieu put his arm round his wife's waist, and tried to rouse himself from his depression; but it had by this time so reacted upon her, that she could not respond to his efforts; and thus the conversation languished, till both felt glad when they reached their destination, which would, at all events, furnish them something to talk about.

Having quitted the carriage and ordered a dinner at the Hôtel de l'Abbaye, the young couple proceeded to visit Mademoiselle de Bellefonds, who was overjoyed to see her sister and new brother-in-law, and doubly so when she found that they had obtained permission to take her out to spend the afternoon with them.

As there is little to be seen at St. Denis but the Abbey, on quitting that part of it devoted to education, they proceeded to visit the church with its various objects of interest; and as De Chaulieu's thoughts were now forced into another direction, his cheerfulness began insensibly to return. Natalie looked so beautiful, too, and the affection betwixt the two young sisters was so pleasant to behold! And they spent a couple of hours wandering about with Hortense, who was almost as well informed as the Suisse, till the brazen doors were open which admitted them to the royal vault.

Satisfied at length with what they had seen, they began to think of returning to the inn, the more especially as De Chaulieu, who had not eaten a morsel of food since the previous evening, confessed to being hungry; so they directed their steps to the door, lingering here and there as they went to inspect a monument or a painting, when happening to turn his head aside to see if his wife, who had stopped to take a last look at the tomb of King Dagobert, was following, he beheld with horror the face of Jacques Rollet appearing from behind a column. At the same instant his wife joined him and took his arm, inquiring if he was not very much delighted with what he had seen. He attempted to say yes, but the word died upon his lips; and staggering out of the door, he alleged that a sudden faintness had overcome him.

They conducted him to the hotel, but Natalie now became seriously alarmed; and well she might. His complexion looked ghastly, his limbs shook, and his features bore an expression of indescribable horror and anguish. What could be the meaning of so extraordinary a change in the gay, witty, prosperous De Chaulieu, who, till that morning, seemed not to have a care in the world? For, plead illness as he might, she felt certain, from the expression of his features, that his sufferings were not of the body, but of the mind; and unable to imagine any reason for such extraordinary manifestations, of which she had never before seen a symptom, but a sudden aversion to herself, and regret for the step he had taken, her pride took the alarm, and, concealing the distress she really felt, she began to assume a haughty and reserved manner toward him, which he naturally interpreted into an evidence of anger and contempt.

The dinner was placed upon the table, but De Chaulieu's appetite, of which he had lately boasted, was quite gone; nor was his wife better able to eat.

The young sister alone did justice to the repast; but although the bridegroom could not eat, he could swallow champagne in such copious draughts that erelong the terror and remorse which the apparition of Jacques Rollet had awakened in his breast were drowned in intoxication.

Amazed and indignant, poor Natalie sat silently observing this elect of her heart, till, overcome with disappointment and grief, she quitted the room with her sister, and retired to another apartment, where she gave free vent to her feelings in tears.

After passing a couple of hours in confidences and lamentations, they recollected that the hours of liberty, granted as an especial favor to Mademoiselle Hortense, had expired; but ashamed to exhibit her husband in his present condition to the eyes of strangers, Natalie prepared to reconduct her to the Maison Royal herself. Looking into the dining-room as they passed, they saw De Chaulieu lying on a sofa, fast asleep, in which state he continued when his wife returned. At length the driver of their carriage begged to know if monsieur and madame were ready to return to Paris, and it became necessary to arouse him.

The transitory effects of the champagne had now subsided; but when De Chaulieu recollected what had happened, nothing could exceed his shame and mortification. So engrossing, indeed, were these sensations, that they quite overpowered his previous ones, and, in his present vexation, he for the moment forgot his fears. He knelt at his wife's feet, begged her pardon a thousand times, swore that he adored her, and declared that the illness and the effect of the wine had been purely the consequences of fasting and overwork.

It was not the easiest thing in the world to reassure a woman whose pride, affection, and taste had been so severely wounded; but Natalie tried to believe, or to appear to do so, and a sort of reconciliation ensued, not quite sincere on the part of the wife, and very humbling on the part of the husband. Under these circumstances it was impossible that he should recover his spirits or facility of manner; his gayety was forced, his tenderness constrained; his heart was heavy within him; and ever and anon the source whence all this disappointment and woe had sprung would recur to his perplexed and tortured mind.

Thus mutually pained and distrustful, they returned to Paris, which they reached about nine o'clock. In spite of her depression, Natalie, who had not seen her new apartments, felt some curiosity about them, whilst De Chaulieu anticipated a triumph in exhibiting the elegant home he had prepared for her. With some alacrity, therefore, they stepped out of the carriage, the gates of the hotel were thrown open, the *concierge* rang the bell which announced to the servants that their master and mistress had arrived; and whilst these domestics appeared above, holding lights over the balusters, Natalie, followed by her husband, ascended the stairs.

But when they reached the landing-place of the first flight, they saw the figure of a man standing in a corner, as if to make way for them. The flash from above fell upon his face, and again Antoine de Chaulieu recognized the features of Jacques Rollet.

From the circumstance of his wife preceding him, the figure was not observed by De Chaulieu till he was lifting his foot to place it on the top stair: the sudden shock caused him to miss the step, and without uttering a sound, he fell back, and never stopped until he reached the stones at the bottom.

The screams of Natalie brought the *concierge* from below and the maids from above, and an attempt was made to raise the unfortunate man from the ground; but with cries of anguish he besought them to desist.

"Let me," he said, "die here. O God! what a dreadful vengeance is thine! Natalie, Natalie," he exclaimed to his wife, who was kneeling beside him, "to win fame, and fortune, and yourself, I committed a dreadful crime. With lying words I argued away the life of a fellow-creature, whom, whilst I uttered them, I half believed to be innocent; and now, when I have attained all I desired and reached the summit of my hopes, the Almighty has sent him back upon the earth to blast me with the sight. Three times this day—three times this day! Again! Again! Again!" And as he spoke, his wild and dilated eyes fixed themselves on one of the individuals that surrounded him.

"He is delirious," said they.

"No," said the stranger, "what he says is true enough, at least in part." And, bending over the expiring man, he added, "May Heaven forgive you, Antoine de Chaulieu! I am no apparition, but the veritable Jacques Rollet, who was saved by one who well knew my innocence. I may name him, for he is beyond the reach of the law now: it was Claperon, the jailer, who, in a fit of jealousy, had himself killed Alphonse de Bellefonds."

"But—but there were three," gasped Antoine.

"Yes, a miserable idiot, who had been so long in confinement for a murder that he was forgotten by the authorities, was substituted for me. At length I obtained, through the assistance of my sister, the position of *concierge* in the Hôtel Marbœuf, in the

Rue Grange Bateliere. I entered on my new place yesterday evening, and was desired to awaken the gentleman on the third floor at seven o'clock. When I entered the room to do so, you were asleep; but before I had time to speak, you awoke, and I recognized your features in the glass. Knowing that I could not vindicate my innocence if you chose to seize me, I fled, and seeing an omnibus starting for St. Denis, I got on it with a vague idea of getting on to Calais and crossing the Channel to England. But having only a franc or two in my pocket, or indeed in the world, I did not know how to procure the means of going forward; and whilst I was lounging about the place, forming first one plan and then another, I saw you in the church, and, concluding that you were in pursuit of me, I thought the best way of eluding your vigilance was to make my way back to Paris as fast as I could; so I set off instantly, and walked all the way; but having no money to pay my night's lodging, I came here to borrow a couple of livres of my sister Claudine, who is a *brodeuse* and resides *au cinquième*."

"Thank Heaven!" exclaimed the dying man, "that sin is off my soul. Natalie, dear wife, farewell! Forgive—forgive all."

These were the last words he uttered; the priest, who had been summoned in haste, held up the cross before his failing sight; a few strong convulsions shook the poor bruised and mangled frame; and then all was still.

Printed in Great Britain
by Amazon